D0062895

First American Edition 2016
Kane Miller, A Division of EDC Publishing

Text, design and illustrations copyright © Lemonfizz Media 2010
First published by Scholastic Australia Pty Limited in 2010
This edition published under license from Scholastic Australia Pty
Limited on behalf of Lemonfizz Media

For information contact:
Kane Miller, A Division of EDC Publishing
P.O. Box 470663
Tulsa, OK 74147-0663
www.kanemiller.com
www.edcpub.com
www.usbornebooksandmore.com

Library of Congress Control Number: 2015953922

Printed and bound in the United States of America
1 2 3 4 5 6 7 8 9 10

ISBN: 978-1-61067-506-2

CHOC SHOCK

SASUAHNN MAFCELARN

Kane Miller
A DIVISION OF EDC PUBLISHING

FRO ADD

Chapter •1

Emma Jacks adored animals. She loved them more than chocolate and that was really saying something. She had a dog, a very fluffy and very cute husky puppy called Pip, and an equally cute but not as fluffy jet-black kitten called Inky. Emma loved Pip and Inky, even though they didn't always love each other.

She did think, however, that there could be a lot more animals in the Jacks family. Although she agreed that a horse was probably unrealistic, she thought that there could be bunnies, budgies, guinea pigs, fish, even frogs... Emma's list of possible pets was long, but her mom's answer was short: no more animals. Emma reminded her mom that when *she* was a little girl she had one dog, five cats, three budgies, two terrapins, eight mice, a dove (which, her mom noted, only stayed while its wing was getting better) and, for a short while, two lambs. Emma's mom said that wasn't the point. Emma rather thought it was.

While she was working on her long-term master plan of persuading her mom to allow her to have more pets, Emma spent a lot of time reading about animals. She read about how to care for them and how to help animals both at home and all over the world. She and her friends Isi, Hannah and Elle had all become junior supporters of the local animal shelter and were planning to do dog walking there when they were a little bit older.

One day all the girls were over at Emma's house. They had taken Pip to the park and had been climbing trees and running everywhere. They were exhausted, but not as exhausted as the little husky, who was now fast asleep on the sofa.

While the girls were having a cold drink, Emma's mom read them an article from the local paper. There had been a fire in the kitchen at the animal shelter. Thankfully, none of the animals had been hurt, but the offices were destroyed. The director of the shelter said that it might have to close if they couldn't raise enough money for the repairs.

"This is awful!" exclaimed Emma. "We have to help. We can't let the shelter close."

"What would happen to all the animals?" asked Elle, looking worried. "We have to do something."

"Maybe we can do something at school?" proposed Hannah. Hannah could always be counted on to have sensible suggestions.

"That is a fantastic idea!" shouted Isi. Isi could always be counted on to be very enthusiastic. "And we have a community service meeting this week."

Emma and Isi were on the school community service committee together. The committee helped plan how the school could raise money to help others. Every class chose two students each year. Emma and Isi were so proud when they were picked—and thrilled that they were picked together. Each year, the committee chose a new project. *Maybe this year it could be saving the animal shelter?* thought Emma. She hoped so.

Emma liked saving things, and she had saved quite a lot already. At least, as Special Agent EJ12 she had.

Emma Jacks, code name EJ12, was a special agent in the under-twelve code-cracking division of the **SHINE** agency. **SHINE** was a secret, international spy agency that stopped evil deeds being done, particularly evil deeds carried out by the *SHADOW* agency. *SHADOW* liked making trouble and making money, ideally both at the same time. *SHADOW* agents were very interested in money and didn't seem to mind how they got it. Or what got damaged when they did. They didn't mind cutting down rain forests if it meant they could build a new spy satellite dish or melting the polar ice cap if they could sell water. Luckily, there were **SHINE** agents to stop them, agents like EJ12.

SHADOW communicated with its evil agents via secret messages. **SHINE** used its agents and clever inventions to intercept those secret messages and then stop the evil plan. *SHADOW* could send messages in nearly everything: texts, emails, letters, even songs. **SHINE** had to be forever on the lookout.

There was also another problem. *SHADOW*'s messages were often in code and that meant **SHINE** needed to be able to decode them. That was where the code-cracking agents came in. **SHINE** didn't mind if some of their agents were quite young. They had a motto (actually they had lots of mottoes, they liked mottoes)—"Judge the agent not the age." They thought their younger agents often gave the grown-ups a real run for their money. Indeed, some of the younger agents, EJ12 included, were their top performers, leading the **SHINE** Shining Stars Spy of the Year competition.

When she was recruited, EJ12 wasn't completely convinced that **SHINE** had made the right decision. But **SHINE** had been right. EJ had stopped lots of *SHADOW* plans. Once she had saved a rain forest, another time she had saved the **SHINE** energy plant. She had also saved baby penguins that were separated from their parents and saved a team of huskies (which is how Pip came to be with Emma). Yes, EJ12 liked saving things and she was good at it.

And now there was the animal shelter, something to save in everyday life. Would she be able to do it as plain, non-secret agent Emma Jacks? She hoped so.

Chapter •2

It was Thursday morning at school and Emma and Isi were sure the clock in their classroom was broken, possibly even going backward. It hardly seemed to be moving at all and they were desperate for the lunch bell to ring. The community service meeting was at lunchtime and they couldn't wait to talk to everyone about the animal shelter.

BWAAAAAAAAHH!

The lunch bell, at last!

The girls grabbed their lunch boxes and rushed toward the library where the meeting was being held. Isi almost ran into Nema on her way. Nema had once been a good friend of Emma's. They had been to kindergarten together and spent lots of time together having fun. But over the last year, Nema had changed. She didn't like doing the stuff she used to like doing. All she seemed to want to do now was flick her hair, a lot, and make up dance routines. And be mean to most people, most of the time. Emma felt sad about that sometimes, but often she just felt cross, especially when Nema was mean to Emma's friends. Emma had learned to stand up to Nema, but sometimes it was better to just ignore her. Today was going to be one of those times.

"Hey, watch it, Dizzy, you nearly knocked me over!" said Nema.

"Oh sorry, Nema," panted Isi, ignoring the fact that Nema had used her nickname in an unfriendly way. "We're just running to the community service meeting."

"It's a community service having you two at the meeting," she said, laughing in her mean, fake laugh.

Emma ignored her. She knew Nema actually

really wanted to be on the committee. The thing was—and everyone realized—that Nema thought the vote was a popularity contest and that's why she wanted to win it. It wasn't though and she didn't. And when Nema didn't get something, well, she would decide that that something wasn't any good anyway and make sure everybody knew it.

Emma and Isi didn't have time for any of that today. They ignored Nema and took off again for the library, where the meeting was just starting. Ms. Tenga, who was Emma and Isi's class teacher, also helped the community service committee. She smiled as two of her most enthusiastic members ran in.

As people ate their lunches, they talked about what projects they might do that year, but when Emma and Isi began telling them about the animal shelter, everyone wanted to talk about that. Everyone wanted to help.

"Okay, it seems we know *who* we want to help," said Ms. Tenga, "so let's talk about *how* we'll do it."

"People could bring a gold coin," suggested Lily.

"We could also have class booths," said Kate, one of the older girls. "It would be like a mini fair."

"Yes! We could cook things and then sell them!" exclaimed Isi. "How much fun would that be!"

"Perhaps we should have a theme," suggested Ms. Tenga.

"Oh, I know!" said Emma, nearly shouting with excitement. "Chocolate!"

"Chocolate what, Emma?" asked Ms. Tenga.

"Chocolate everything!" replied Emma. "We could have a Chocolate Lovers' Day!"

It was unanimous. After all, who doesn't love chocolate? Every class had to make something, anything at all, as long as it contained chocolate.

When Emma and Isi went back to their class after lunch and told them about Chocolate Lovers' Day, everyone was excited. The class decided to make cupcakes—chocolate cupcakes.

Isi, being Isi, was perhaps the most excited. "How good is this, Em?" she cried. "Helping animals and eating chocolate! Does it get any better?" Before Emma could answer, Isi started talking again.

"Hold on, it *can* get better!" Isi cried. "Let's make the cupcakes together! I'll ask my mom if you can come for a sleepover so we can practice this weekend. See—helping animals, eating chocolate *and* having a sleepover!"

Emma smiled at her slightly crazy friend. She had to agree with her.

Early the next Saturday at Isi's house, Isi and Emma were in their pajamas, trying to find a good cupcake recipe.

"Imagine if we could make this one," said Isi. She was looking in a magazine at an ad for Madame Ombre's Chocolate Cake Sensations shop. Madame Ombre was a celebrity chef and famous chocolate baker, known all around the world for her signature cake, the Triple Chocolate Ripple and Chocolate Chip Mousse Cupcake. It was the ultimate chocolate cupcake. It started with dark, dark chocolate at the base working to a milk chocolate center and then a white chocolate peak. Each layer had chocolate ripple mixed through it and, if all this was not enough, the center of the cupcake was hollowed out and then filled with chocolate mousse. As a final touch on an already ridiculously chocolatey cake, there was chocolate icing with three wedges of chocolate—one dark, one milk and one white—arranged on the top.

"Imagine how much money we could raise if we made these," said Isi.

"You don't think they might be a little bit complicated for us?" said Emma, who also wondered if it would be wrong to have a poster of a cupcake on your wall. "And anyway, the recipe is top secret. Madame Ombre has never written it down or told it to anyone."

Isi giggled. "We could try making it up."

"Maybe," said Emma, still flicking through pages in a way that she hoped said "maybe not at all."

"Knock knock," said Isi randomly.

"Huh?" said Emma. "Oh, I get it. Who's there?"

"Imogen," replied Isi.

"Imogen who?"

"Imogen a life without chocolate!" shrieked Isi.

Emma laughed, then saw something in the cookbook. "Hey, how about this one, Is? 'Really Simple Double-chocolate Cupcakes.'"

"That sounds more like us," said Isi. "I know! We could decorate the cupcakes to look like cats and dogs, and use chocolate chips for eyes and icing to make whiskers!"

The fact that neither Isi nor Emma had made cupcakes before didn't worry her in the slightest. In fact, Isi saw that as an exciting challenge rather than a problem. Emma loved the way her friend could do that and was a little bit jealous. Emma seemed better at thinking about the things that could go wrong, so much so that sometimes she could convince herself not to do something at all. In fact, she was just starting to think that whiskers might be rather tricky when her friend interrupted her thoughts.

"What are we waiting for?" said Isi with her head halfway into one of the kitchen cupboards. "I know there's a bowl here somewhere."

The girls got out the ingredients and got started.

The recipe may have been called "really simple," but they had a few problems. Isi's mom looked less and less excited about the whole project as more and more sugar, flour and chocolate ended up on the girls, the kitchen counter, the floor, even on Isi's younger brother's diaper. Some batter, however, had stayed in the bowl and was ready to go into the cupcake pans. Or was it?

"Hey, Is," said Emma, checking the recipe. "It says to beat the batter until smooth."

"Hmm," said Isi, spooning through the batter a bit.

"What does 'hmm' mean?" asked Emma looking up from the book, a little worried.

"It means 'hmm, our batter isn't very smooth,'" replied Isi, giggling.

"Isi, that's not funny," said Emma a little too crossly. "We might have ruined the whole thing."

"Lighten up, Em!" said Isi. "A few lumps will be fine. Don't stress. We can call them Chocolate Surprise Cakes with surprise lumps of chocolate in every one!"

"Hmm," said Emma, but her hmm was grumpier than Isi's had been.

Emma was good at lots of things, but "winging it," going with the flow and seeing what happened, wasn't one of them. She liked things to be planned; she liked things to turn out as they were supposed to turn out. Like math. Twelve times ten would always be 120, and 354 plus 122 would always be 476. That was why she liked numbers so much and it was why she didn't like unexpected things, things like a cupcake batter that was supposed to be smooth having lumps in it.

"Oh no, now these look really weird!" cried Emma, as she spooned some batter into the cupcake pans.

"Well, maybe a little, Em, but they'll taste yum and we've had fun doing it," said Isi, licking her chocolatey fingers. "Don't beat yourself up. Hey, do you get it: beat yourself up, beating the batter! I'm a riot!"

Emma smiled at her friend's bad joke and stopped thinking about the lumpy cupcakes. "I get it, Isi, I get it!"

"Well, anyway, it's not worth getting upset over,

like it's something really important," Isi went on. "We don't have to decorate them as cats and dogs."

Isi is right, thought Emma, *some things are more important than others.* And she knew that her friend knew what she was talking about. Isi's rabbit had died a few months before and *that* was something to get upset over. Back then Isi hadn't been her normal bouncy self for a while. Now Emma felt silly as well as cross about the cupcakes. Luckily her friend knew a quick way to cheer her up.

"Come on, let's get Mom to help us put these in the oven. Then we can lick the bowl and watch some TV while they bake."

Licking the bowl. That lightened Emma's mood. A lot.

Little did she know that Isi and her cupcakes weren't the only things heating up. Evil agency *SHADOW* was also cooking up something, something a lot worse than a few lumpy chocolate cupcakes.

Chapter 3

"And now, a special word from Madame Ombre…"

The girls had changed out of their pajamas and were watching TV when an ad came on for Madame Ombre's hugely popular cooking competition show, "Choc Chef." Contestants on the show would come to Madame Ombre's bakery and compete for the title of Choc Chef.

"*Bonjour,* friends of *chocolat,* as we say in France," said Madame Ombre, a tall, skinny and slightly cross-looking woman. Emma wondered how you could possibly look cross when you baked chocolate cakes all day. Madame Ombre's black hair was tied back in a severe bun, largely hidden under a tall chef's hat. Her small, dark eyes peered out over thin black-rimmed glasses that perched on the top of her long, narrow nose.

"Today is an exciting day. It is the finals of a special Junior Choc Chef competition to be held in my chocolate bakery. The lucky finalists will receive a tour of my bakery and compete in my kitchen for the title of Junior Choc Chef of the Year, announced live on TV tonight. *C'est magnifique!*"

"*C'est* cool!" cried Isi. "I wish we had entered. Imagine going inside Madame Ombre's bakery. It would be like Willy Wonka's factory!"

Emma thought of the globby batter spilling over the pan in the oven. "Don't take this the wrong way, Is," said Emma, "but I'm not so sure we would have made it to the finals."

"You may be right," said Isi, smiling. "The world may not quite be ready for our Chocolate Surprise Cakes."

Ping!

It was the oven timer. The world might not be

ready for them, but the first batch of cupcakes was ready to come out of the oven.

Piinngg!

That ping didn't come from the oven, thought Emma. *It came from my phone.* It was no ordinary phone and no ordinary ping—it was a mission alert from SHINE.

Emma's phone was one of the best things about being a SHINE agent. Sure, saving the world was better, but Emma's special SHINE-issue phone was very, very good. It was a cross between a game console and a mobile phone, which was handy if you needed to pretend you were a normal girl playing a game when really you were a secret agent using one of the phone's many spy applications. There were apps to identify wild animals, apps to find your way around strange countries and, of course, apps to help agents crack codes. There wasn't, however, an app to tell you how to report in for a mission if your normal reporting drill took place at school and you received a mission alert while at a friend's house. Which was exactly what had just happened. Emma would normally respond to a mission alert by entering the **SHINE** Mission Tube, an underground secret transportation system, and she normally accessed the Mission Tube via the girls' bathroom at school. Starting a mission in the bathroom could be embarrassing, but it got Emma to the Mission Tube fast. How was she going to do that from Isi's house?

Just as Emma was starting to worry about what to do, Isi's mom came into the room.

"Emma, your mom just called. Something's come up at home and she needs you back early. She is on her way to pick you up."

"Oh no, we haven't even begun to decorate the cakes," cried Isi.

But Emma was relieved. She knew what her mom was up to—sometimes it was pretty useful having a mom who also used to be a secret agent for **SHINE**.

"Lighten up, Isi!" said Emma, smiling at her friend.

Isi stuck her tongue out at Emma and laughed.

Emma's mom arrived quickly and they were soon in the car and heading off.

"This isn't the way to school, Mom," said Emma, thinking that maybe her mom was not such a good ex-agent after all.

"We're not going to school," replied Emma's mom. "**SHINE** has requested you report to the Light Shop. It will be opening in five minutes and we'll be arriving there in six."

Emma took back her thought about her mom not being a very good ex-agent.

"And here we are: the Light Shop."

"Okay, Mom, thanks," said Emma, opening the car door.

"Oh, don't forget to ask the lady if they have any new lights!" called her mom, as she pulled out from the curb and drove away.

Emma turned back to the Light Shop, an ordinary-looking shop in an ordinary-looking shopping street selling ordinary-looking lights. "We **SHINE** a light!" said the sign in the window and Emma smiled because she knew that was also one of the many **SHINE** mottoes, with two small but important words left off—"We shine a light on evil." Which is what, twenty floors down in their underground headquarters, **SHINE** did.

Emma pushed open the door and a buzzer went off. She walked up to the desk at the back of the shop where an elderly lady was sitting reading a book. As EJ approached, the lady looked up, smiling.

"Hello," she said.

"Hello," replied Emma.

The lady looked back down at her book.

Hang on, that's not right, thought EJ. *Oh, what was it Mom said? Yes, I remember now.* EJ coughed to clear her throat and looked at the lady again.

"Excuse me, do you have any new lights that you can show me?"

"Yes we do, indeed we do!" cried the woman. "Well done, that was the password. Please put your hand on here," said the lady, smiling as she placed a small black box in front of EJ.

EJ put her hand on the pad, which buzzed for a moment, then stopped. A small green light on the side of the box glowed.

"You are cleared for access, EJ12," said the lady. "Please take the elevator to level 20 and await further instructions. Good luck—and I hope you like chocolate, EJ12!"

Chocolate? A mission with chocolate? Could it be true? EJ12 hoped so.

Chapter • 4

The elevator stopped at level 20. EJ waited. A digital voice started talking.

"Welcome, Agent EJ12. Exit elevator and turn left. Continue until you come to the Code Room."

EJ walked until she came to a plain metal door with a small keypad and screen next to it. EJ knew the drill. She keyed in her pin code and another digital voice began talking.

"Security test commencing. Knock knock."

Knock knock? This was new. **SHINE** always had new ways of confirming an agent's identity, but was this really a knock-knock joke? There was nothing for it, EJ had to answer.

"Who's there?"

"Agent."

It is a knock-knock joke, thought Emma.

"Agent Who?" she answered.

"Agent EJ12, welcome, voice and sense of humor recognition complete. Door open."

Very funny, thought EJ, as she went into the room. Isi would have liked that one.

The Code Room at HQ was a small, simple, yellow-painted room with a chair, a table with SHINE-issue paper and pen, and a long, clear tube coming from the ceiling directly over the table. The messages came via the tube and EJ sat and waited until a little capsule came whooshing down. EJ took the capsule and unscrewed the lid. She pulled out a memory stick.

I kind of expected a coded message, thought EJ. *Maybe it's on this.* She plugged the stick into her phone.

A message came up on her screen.

FOR EJ'S EYES ONLY.

DVD INTERCEPTED EN ROUTE

TO A KNOWN SHADOW AGENT 8.47AM.

SENT TO EJI2 10.04AM.

ASSESS FOOTAGE FOR POSSIBLE

MESSAGE.

Then EJ's screen went black for a moment before a part of an episode of Madame Ombre's "Choc Chef" came on. *Was there a mistake?* wondered EJ.

It was a cooking segment, showing how to decorate cupcakes. Madame Ombre was using chocolate drops and sprinkles, tiny flowers and silver balls, lots of lovely things, all to make the most beautifully decorated cupcakes.

"I call these Mixed-Up Surprises, and to make them you must first make perfect cakes," said Madame Ombre. "They must be light and fluffy and perfectly smooth."

EJ thought back to her and Isi's Chocolate Surprise Cakes and winced as she saw how different two "surprise" cakes could be. She could not, however, see what the segment might have to do with SHINE. She watched it again, and then again, trying to spot why *SHADOW* would be sending this to one of their agents. She also checked her watch to see how long she had taken. SHINE kept records of how quickly their agents cracked messages and EJ wanted to do well. She couldn't crack a message she couldn't see though, could she?

Then, on the fourth watching, EJ noticed something. There was one tray of cupcakes already decorated on Madame Ombre's workstation and they all had chocolate drops on them, little chocolate drops with letters on them. Was it just a half-baked idea or was there a message on those cupcakes? EJ paused the video on the bit where she could best see the tray and looked closely at the chocolate drops on each cupcake, copying down on a piece of paper what she saw.

6S SKCAE YARED FATRE RJN HOCC HFEC DSEN LSFKEA

It has to be a message, thought EJ. Why else would you have such a random collection of letters on top of the cakes, unless they weren't random at all but rather a coded message! EJ looked at the "words." Could it be a backward code? She tried that.

S6 EACKS DERAY ERTAF

EJ didn't need to go on, it clearly wasn't a backward code. *Hold on,* EJ thought, *hadn't Madame Ombre called these cakes "Mixed-Up Surprises"? Was that a hint? Were the letters all mixed up?* EJ looked to see if she could un-jumble them.

6S CAKES READY AFTER JNR CHOC CHEF SEND FLAKES

EJ smiled as she wrote the decoded message down on a piece of paper, put the paper back in the capsule and pushed the capsule up the tube. There was a whoosh as the capsule was sucked up and away to the briefing room, where A1, the head of **SHINE**, would be waiting for it—and for EJ12.

Chapter · 5

Piinngg! There was another message on EJ's phone.

> RETURN TO LIFT
> PRESS NUMBERS 8
> AND 17

EJ wondered why she needed to press two buttons for one floor. Then the elevator stopped. As the elevator doors opened, EJ saw a small sign with just two letters on the two metal doors across the corridor from the elevator: HQ.

Now I get it, a simple letter-number match, 8 = H and 17 = Q, thought EJ, as the two doors slid open. *Gee whizz, lemonfizz, SHINE likes codes.*

"Yes we do, EJ12, and welcome back to SHINE," said an older woman standing in front of EJ as the doors opened to the SHINE operations room.

EJ smiled. It was A1, head of SHINE. A1 was, as always, wearing a smart black suit, crisp white shirt and a long chain around her neck with a beautiful, large yellow pendant that almost glowed hanging from it. EJ wondered what sort of stone it was.

"It is a rare sapphire," said A1, who had a slightly unnerving habit of seeming to know what you were thinking. "Most people think sapphires are only blue, but they can be all sorts of colors. Now, we have work to do, EJ. Let's take a look at the message." A1 turned, and as she did so said, "Light Screen lower."

She and EJ watched as an enormous plasma screen came down from the high ceiling of the operations room. It was the SHINE Light Screen and with it you could find out almost anything you wanted or needed to know. Through the Light Screen you could access the Internet and, if you had the right security clearance, the entire **SHINE** network of files. The Light Screen was voice activated and touch sensitive, and you could move screens around and call up new ones by command.

"Show message," instructed A1. Almost immediately, the message EJ had written in the Code Room flashed up on the screen.

DVD INTERCEPTED EN ROUTE TO A
KNOWN SHADOW AGENT 8.47AM.
SENT TO EJI2 10.04AM.
ASSESS FOOTAGE FOR POSSIBLE
MESSAGE.
TIME TAKEN TO DECODE 0.33
65 CAKES READY AFTER JNR CHOC
CHEF SEND FLAKES

"Well done on finding the message, EJ," said A1. "Finding *and* decoding the message in just over half an hour, that is impressive."

EJ blushed. "Thanks, A1, but I don't know what the message means."

"We can help with that, or at least some of it." A1 turned back to face the Light Screen. "Show files on *SHADOW* S6."

Images flooded the screen, images of codes and of tiny gadgets.

"What are they?" asked EJ.

"We are not completely sure," replied A1, "but we think they may be early prototypes of something called S6."

"Oh," said EJ, beginning to blush again, "so it isn't 6S."

"No, I don't think so, but that doesn't matter. In fact, it's six of one and half a dozen of the other," said A1, laughing at her own little joke. "Either way it means the same thing. It's just that we have seen other messages about S6." A1 looked at the screen again. "Light Screen change 6S to S6," she said. "We know, EJ, that S6 stands for *SHADOW* Secret Scramble Send and Spy System. It is a new code-making machine, a machine that makes codes that are nearly impossible to crack. Our top code professor has been working on S6 and she is the best person to brief you." A1 turned again to the screen. "Light Screen, teleconference Agent CO45."

There were a few beeps and then an image of a young woman in a white scientist's coat and with slightly crazy, long curly red hair came onto the Light Screen.

"Good morning, A1. Good morning, EJ12, nice to meet you."

"Hello, CO45," said EJ, smiling. She wondered if it was just a coincidence that if you used a simple alphabet-number match, starting with A being 1, 4 and 5 would make the scientist's code name CODE. She thought not.

"What can you tell us about S6?" said A1.

"It's clever," said CO45. "I wish we had invented it, but actually *SHADOW* didn't invent it either. They have really only created a smaller, digital version of a powerful code-making machine used more than fifty years ago. It was called the Enigma machine and it produced codes that seemed completely random, making them almost impossible to crack. We think *SHADOW* has created a modern version to communicate with their agents. We also believe they have developed it in such a way that they can send it out in small parts their agents can assemble. Ingenious really."

"But if they do that," said EJ, "we won't be able to crack their messages. And if we can't crack their messages, we won't be able to stop their plans."

"Exactly, EJ12," said CO45, nodding. "But, luckily, they haven't quite finished it. At least, that's what we thought until you found their latest message on the cupcakes. And," CO45 added, "were you aware that '*Ombre*' is French for 'shadow'? I think that and the fact that she is sending out this message confirms that she is working for *SHADOW*."

"Indeed. Good work, CO45. Thank you for your time."

"My pleasure, A1. CO45 out."

"So what do we know?" said A1 to EJ, as the decoded message appeared again on the screen.

```
65 CAKES READY AFTER JNR
CHOC CHEF SEND FLAKES
```

"S6 has to be the *SHADOW* code machine, but I'm not sure what S6 cakes are," said EJ. "And Jnr Choc Chef has to be the Junior Choc Chef finals that are on today," she added, remembering the TV ad she and Isi had seen earlier. "They are being held in Madame Ombre's bakery."

"Well done, EJ," said A1. "So, there are some cakes that have something to do with S6 and they will be ready after the competition. We can assume Madame Ombre has baked them and now, it seems, she wants *SHADOW* to send flakes."

"But what are flakes?" asked EJ. "Decorations?"

"Maybe, but we don't know," said A1. "We have, however, had our suspicions about Madame Ombre and her chocolate cake bakery for some time. In fact, we have had an agent from the surveillance division in the bakery for the last couple of weeks."

"I didn't know we had a surveillance division," said EJ.

"All **SHINE** information is on a strictly NTK—need-to-know—basis, EJ, and up until now you have not needed to know about it, but now you do. The agents in the surveillance division are highly trained not only in watching but also in hiding. They have to spend long amounts of time in some very strange and often very small places while they keep an eye on targets."

"I bet they are good at hide-and-seek," said EJ.

A1 laughed. "Actually, that is one of the ways we choose these agents, EJ. Anyway, back to business. Each day we have sent an agent, CC12, into the bakery. She has then found herself a hiding place and watched. She comes out a few hours later with the garbage truck—after all, we can't let our agents fall behind in their schoolwork. Agent CC12 has confirmed that there has been much more baking than usual, a lot even by Madame Ombre's standards."

"Baking of what?" asked EJ.

"That's what we need to find out, EJ, and quickly," replied A1. "It is time to get you into that bakery."

"But how?" said EJ.

"Congratulations!" said A1 suddenly.

"I beg your pardon, A1," said EJ.

"Congratulations, EJ," repeated A1, "or should that be Emma Sekac, which is your undercover name for this mission?"

"I get it," said EJ after a moment, "s-e-k-a-c is c-a-k-e-s backward, but why undercover?"

"Because," said A1, "you, Emma Sekac, are the surprise late entrant in the Junior Choc Chef finals!"

Uh-oh, I really don't think I am the right agent for this mission, thought EJ. *I'll have to tell A1 about Isi's and my Chocolate Surprise Cakes!*

Chapter • 6

"Now, EJ, I know you haven't had a lot of cooking experience," said A1, "but it is all about a lightness of touch. Don't let a few lumpy cakes get you down."

How does she do that? wondered EJ. *And "don't let a few lumpy cakes get you down"—that's easy for you to say!* EJ didn't think A1 would stress about anything.

"We have some charms that I think should help as well," continued A1.

EJ smiled at that. Charm was actually CHARM, Clever Hidden Accessories with Release Mechanism.

The **SHINE** inventors would invent all kinds of useful gadgets and tools for agents to use on missions and then shrink them to the size of small charms— spy charms. The **SHINE** agents wore the charms on a special bracelet. When they needed to, they twisted the charm to release it to its normal size so it could work. There were four charms laid out on the table: a whisk, a heart, a cupcake and a chocolate bar. EJ was particularly interested in the last two.

"This one is hard to beat," said A1, holding the whisk charm. "The **SHINE** whisk-o-matic guarantees beautiful, light and fluffy cakes every time and also tests and adjusts for perfect flavor, thanks to its hidden computer chip. That should help you stand out in the Junior Choc Chef finals. But this one," A1 continued, holding up another little charm, "this is really the icing on the cake. It is a triumph, it is a…"

"Cupcake?" said EJ.

"Yes, EJ, a cupcake," said A1 smiling. "But this is not a real cupcake. It is cupcake-cam, the world's first flip-top cake and possibly the most ingenious creation yet from our **SHINE** inventor-in-chief, IQ400."

"How does it work?" asked EJ.

"You simply twist, as usual," explained A1, "and then wait for the cupcake to enlarge." She demonstrated. "There we are. Now, you see this cherry on top? It is no ordinary cherry, it is a tiny camera. You simply leave the cherry in a position where you want to film and press the little button on the side to start filming. To watch, you simply flip back the top of the cupcake. Underneath is a little screen. The film will be transmitted back to you on the cupcake-cam."

"Sweet!" said EJ.

"Indeed. EJ, as we are short of time, you will be briefed on the choc charm on the way to the bakery."

EJ looked forward to that one. She was really hoping the choc charm was going to involve eating chocolate.

"But what about Agent CC12?" asked EJ. "How will I contact her?"

"She will contact you," replied A1. "That is the best way to protect whatever hiding spot she has chosen. You will, however, need a special password sequence so you both know you are who you say you are. I will show you that now," said A1, as she turned to the Light Screen. "Light Screen, show password sequence."

EJ looked at the screen and read the rather odd exchange that appeared there.

Agent 1: I like chocolate very much, do you?

Agent 2: Oh yes, especially white chocolate—have you tried it with grated carrot?

Agent 1: No, I have only had it with tomato. I hope to try carrot soon.

Agent 2: Yes, you must.

"I am going to say that?" asked EJ.

"I know it's a little silly," said A1 "but that helps make sure no one else would say it by accident. Now EJ, memorize the exchange."

EJ reread the password sequence.

"Have you done that?"

EJ nodded.

"Excellent," said A1, turning toward the screen. "Light Screen, delete exchange," she said, turning back to face EJ. "Remember: the exchange must be exactly those words." She held out the charms to EJ. "Now, EJ, here are your charms," said A1. "You will need to add them to your bracelet and get changed. Your outfit is in the dressing room. Please put the clothes you are wearing in the bag provided and bring it with you when you are ready."

EJ went to the dressing room and smiled when she saw a chef's outfit hanging up—blue-checkered pants and a white jacket with white buttons on each side. As a finishing touch there was a chef's hat and a red-and-white checkered scarf. They were just like the ones the contestants wore on "Choc Chef."

How does SHINE get all these things? wondered EJ.

EJ quickly got changed. The outfit, as always, fit her perfectly. She attached her new charms to her bracelet and came out of the dressing room with her normal clothes in the bag.

"Perfect!" declared A1. "You look ready, EJ, or should I say Emma Sekac. Now, let's get you to that chocolate bakery."

"What should I do with this, A1?" asked EJ, holding up the bag of clothes.

"Oh, you can give them to your mom," replied A1.

Mom? thought EJ.

"Yes, your mom. She is waiting outside to take you to the Choc Chef competition."

"Oh," said EJ, both a little surprised and disappointed. EJ loved her mom, but, really, what sort of secret agent was taken to a mission by her mother?

Chapter • 7

EJ had traveled to and from missions in some pretty unusual ways. She had parachuted out of planes, crossed seas in icebreakers, flown in helicopters and even been chauffeured in a limousine. But this time was different. As Emma opened the door of the Light Shop out into the street, there was her mother in the front seat of the family car with the window down, smiling. It was just like when Emma's mom picked her up from school, gymnastics and her friends' homes, but nothing like the start of a mission.

"Hop in, Special Agent EJ12," said her mom.

"Just EJ's fine, Mom," said EJ.

"Oh, okay then. Well, EJ, put your seat belt on and let's go."

"Aaarrggh," groaned EJ, as she wondered how many other agents were reminded to put their seat belts on. Then EJ noticed a small yellow button on the steering wheel. She was sure that hadn't been there when her mom dropped her off.

"Has that yellow button always been there, Mom?" asked EJ.

"No, it's new. I had it put in at the Shiny Car Wash down the road while you were having your briefing," replied EJ's mom. "And, thanks for reminding me, darling: I need to push it and you need to open the glove compartment and put your headphones on."

And with that, EJ's mom pressed the button. EJ opened the glove compartment. Nothing was there except the hair tie she had accused her brother, Bob, of stealing.

"Mom?" said EJ.

"Give it a chance to warm up," replied her mom.

Seconds later, there was a beep and the panel at the back of the glove compartment slid back revealing a small screen that moved forward. On the screen was the **SHINE** logo.

PRESS SCREEN TO SELECT OPTION:

AGENT TRAINING EXERCISES

IN-CAR ENTERTAINMENT

MAPS

MISSION BRIEFING

This is cool, thought EJ. She and her brother had always thought they should have a TV in the car. It was one of the few things they agreed on. EJ wondered whether they would be allowed to use it on normal trips.

"Mom," said EJ, "I was just wondering..."

"No, we can't," replied her mom. "You know

the rules. All equipment is strictly for mission use only. Now put those headphones on and have your briefing."

EJ sighed as she plugged in the headphones and pressed Mission Briefing on the screen. As she did, the screen flickered and then A1 appeared on screen.

"Hello again, EJ12. Let us recap. We believe *SHADOW* has invented a device, which they call S6, to create unbreakable codes and that they are preparing to distribute S6 to their agent network. Madame Ombre, the world-famous chocolate baker, seems mixed up in all this. The message you found indicates something is about to happen at her bakery. Your mission, EJ12, is to enter the bakery as one of the Junior Choc Chef finalists and find out exactly what Madame Ombre is up to. To do that, you are going to have to make sure you get through to the final."

Aarrggh, thought EJ. *How am I going to make it to the final of Junior Choc Chef? I can't even make simple chocolate cupcakes. **SHINE** couldn't have* *picked someone more hopeless for this mission!*

"You are perfect for this mission," continued A1, "and we expect great work. Now, let's review the choc charm."

Yes! thought EJ, thinking the choc charm had to be something fabulous, perhaps something that involved an endless supply of chocolate.

"The choc charm isn't chocolate at all," continued A1.

Oh, sighed EJ, *what a pity.*

"Inside what looks like a chocolate bar is a tiny bugging device, so you can listen in on conversations without detection. Once you have activated the charm by twisting it you will be holding what looks like four rows of chocolate. Two rows hold the listening device and the other two rows hold the receiving device. Simply leave the listening pieces where your suspect will be talking and switch it on. You will then be able to hear through the other two rows."

"Right," said EJ, still a little disappointed that there was no actual chocolate connected with the charm.

"Finally, EJ12," continued A1, "as always, you are going to need some help on this mission. You will make contact with Agent CC12, but also ensure you upload your BESTie before you arrive at the bakery. And now I think you'd better switch to the GPS function. Your mother has just taken a wrong turn, if I am not mistaken. **SHINE** out."

A1 is never mistaken, thought EJ. The menu screen reappeared and she pressed Maps. She then pressed Location and keyed in the address of the bakery. Almost immediately a bossy voice instructed them to make an immediate U-turn. While her mom, looking slightly stressed, turned the car in the opposite direction, EJ took out her phone and pressed the BESTie app.

SHINE knew that agents worked better when they had the support of others, and had created the Brains, Expertise, Support and Tips network, known as BESTies, to help agents on missions. Each agent had a list of trusted friends or family members who had been screened by **SHINE** and authorized for mission assist. An agent could upload one BESTie for each mission and that person would be on standby to help her.

EJ decided to upload Isi—she may not have been the greatest cook (in fact, she may have been one of the worst), but she was very good at keeping things light and relaxed. *In the pressure cooker conditions of the Junior Choc Chef finals, and for an important mission, that will be just what I need,* EJ thought. She touched Isi's picture on her phone screen, activating the system that would send her friend an alert message.

"Nearly there," said her mom, turning another corner.

EJ looked out the car window. She could see the bakery, a large brown building surrounded by a tall iron fence with two large gates at the front. If you looked closely, you could see that iron cupcakes were on the top of each of the fence posts. And outside the gate stood a group of kids, all wearing the same chef's uniforms. The Junior Choc Chef finalists.

"Well, this is it, EJ," said her mom, as they pulled

up outside the gates. "Good luck and don't eat too much chocolate!"

"I won't, Mom," cried EJ, as she got out of the car. EJ felt calm as she headed toward the gates.

That wasn't going to last long.

Chapter •8

EJ joined the end of the line of Junior Choc Chefs just as Madame Ombre began to speak. She was also dressed in chef's clothes, but rather than white, they were black with some beautiful white lettering stitched on her jacket.

Madame Ombre
"First comes chocolate"

Well, you have to agree with that, thought EJ.
"Bonjour tout le monde! I am Madame Ombre,

the great, if I may say so myself—the truly great chocolate baker. Welcome *mes petites* Choc Chefs, welcome to the Junior Choc Chef final. You are all very lucky to be here, are you not?"

Some luckier than others, thought EJ, who was wondering how she was going to pull off pretending she could cook.

"As you all know, my signature cake is the exquisite Triple Chocolate Ripple and Chocolate Chip Mousse Cupcake. We will commence with each of you telling me about the cake that got you to the Junior Choc Chef finals."

EJ gulped as Madame Ombre made her way down the line of contestants. She had to think quickly.

"I prepared a white and dark chocolate soufflé," declared one girl proudly.

"I created chocolate éclairs with white chocolate cream," said another, beaming.

Gee whizz, lemonfizz, thought EJ, *doesn't anyone here just make simple cakes? I will be lucky to make it to the kitchen let alone the final.*

I can hardly say that I created lumpy batter that oozed all over the oven! But I'd better come up with something.

"I made a chocolate mousse tart with triple chocolate curls," said the girl next to EJ.

"And you," said Madame Ombre, looking at EJ over the top of her glasses. "What was *your* winning chocolate creation?"

"I made Chocolate Surprise," said EJ, trying to sound as confident as the other contestants.

"Hmm, Chocolate Surprise, I do not know this one," said Madame Ombre. "Tell me…"

Ring!

"Ah, the bell!" exclaimed Madame Ombre.

EJ swallowed. A very loud bell had saved her, for now anyway. That was close.

Madame Ombre waved her hand. "Enough chitty chatty. We will now enter my bakery. I will first give you a *petite* tour and then we go to my master kitchen where the competition will commence. Don't dawdle!"

Excellent, a tour, thought EJ. *The perfect opportunity to look around the bakery and see what I can find out.*

"Come along, keep up," cried Madame Ombre. With long strides she led the ten contestants through the gates and up the steps of the bakery. It was difficult to keep up with her. They entered a long corridor and already there was a warm, sweet smell in the air. "First stop, the chocolate room," cried Madame Ombre.

That got everyone moving, and the contestants almost ran after Madame Ombre until she stopped outside a door.

"Here is where the chocolate for my cakes is prepared and stored," said Madame Ombre. She opened the door to reveal three enormous chocolate fountains, one flowing with white chocolate, one with milk chocolate and one with dark chocolate. In each fountain, chocolate cascaded down three tiers before falling into a large vat that swirled the chocolate around and around. There was a little gold tap on the side of each vat.

"The fountain keeps the chocolate moving, making it light and fluffy," explained Madame Ombre. "Here, you may try," and she took some plastic cups and filled them with a little of the milk chocolate before passing one to each contestant.

Trying to look professional, EJ took a sip. It was the smoothest, creamiest chocolate she had ever tasted. It was more than delicious. It was so good that she couldn't help drinking the rest down in a few gulps.

"C'est magnifique, non?" said Madame Ombre. "And no lumps. I can't have lumps, I detest lumps. I need lightness and lightness only in my chocolate

cakes and for my chocolate icing. But let us keep moving. No chitty chatty, quick, quick."

And with that EJ and the group reluctantly left the chocolate room and walked back into and down the corridor until they arrived at another door.

M.O.C.B.

Chocolate Sculpting

"Ah," sighed Madame Ombre. "Here is where we create the models that we use in our theme cakes. Perhaps it will be a little white chocolate fairy on a pink-iced cupcake with tiny yellow flowers? Or maybe some little bunnies on my Easter egg cupcake? Here is where my chefs design the shapes and create the molds. Come quietly and watch."

Madame Ombre opened the door to what looked more like a craft class than a kitchen. There was a group of chefs, all dressed in the same black outfit as Madame Ombre but without her chef hat. They were sitting at pottery wheels working with clay. As EJ and the rest of the group moved closer, they could see that the chefs were molding little rabbits and, on a little podium in front of them all, were six live rabbits. The rabbits had tight collars around their necks and leashes tying them to the podium so that they wouldn't escape.

"Today," continued Madame Ombre, "my trainee chefs are learning to create perfect Easter bunny chocolates. To do this, they must study real bunnies."

EJ looked at the bunnies tied to the podium and felt sorry for them. "Excuse me, Madame Ombre, but do the bunnies like being inside?"

"What?" said Madame Ombre.

"The rabbits," said another girl, smiling at EJ. "Do the rabbits like being kept as models?"

"Oh, them. I do not know, I do not care," said Madame Ombre, giving a little shrug. "What is that to me? They are only rabbits. The chocolate bunnies on my Easter cakes must be perfect."

EJ stared at Madame Ombre in surprise, as

did many of the other contestants. *Is nothing more important to her than her chocolate cakes?* EJ wondered. *Is that why she is working with SHADOW? Are they giving her something she wants for her chocolate cakes? Something she can't get herself?*

"Enough of the bunnies. We have one more room to see before we commence our competition. Out now, enough chitty chatty."

Once again the group bustled out of the room and into the corridor. The next door they came to was not the same plain door as the others. This one was festooned with ribbons, tiny bells, flowers, streamers, balloons and even twinkling lights. EJ was not surprised when she read the sign on the door.

M.O.C.B.

Decorating Room

"And this, this is where we make every cake a party!" cried Madame Ombre. "The cake itself is merely a base, a delicious canvas on which to paint a story, and in here are the ingredients for those paintings."

With a flourish, Madame Ombre opened the door to a room lined with shelves stacked with glass jars. All of them were filled with the most beautiful and delicious little things you could imagine putting on a cake. There were sprinkles and jelly beans, a jar for every color and shade. There were silver balls, gold balls, chocolate balls, gummy snakes, gummy bears, tiny sugar flowers, licorice, chocolate drops, chocolate curls, chocolate stars and candy canes. There was candy fruit: bananas, cherries, pineapples, pears and even tiny, tiny watermelons. There were tubes of icing and marshmallows of different sizes and colors. Then there were the little figurines and objects, some in chocolate, some in marzipan, of fairies, guitars and pianos, soccer players, brides and grooms and animals, including the chocolate bunnies.

"Some of you will have a chance to use these decorations in the final, but who?" declared Madame Ombre, as she closed the door. "And so, off to the Choc Chef kitchen!"

Just before they reached the kitchen, which was at the end of the corridor, they passed one more door, a plain door with plain writing.

M.O.C.B.
Storeroom

"Excuse me, Madame Ombre," EJ called out, "may we look in this room?"

"*Non!* Don't go in there!" shouted Madame Ombre. "No one, no one but *moi* ever enters."

And me, said EJ12 to herself. She knew she would have to get inside that room.

But first she was going to have to bake the best cakes of her short, and so far unsuccessful, cooking career. Could she do it?

Chapter • 9

The competition was about to begin. Madame Ombre had led the junior choc chefs into the huge bakery kitchen where there was a workstation for each contestant. EJ's was at the front of the room. Each workstation was laid out with ingredients, had a cupboard underneath holding pots and pans and held a stove and oven.

Madame Ombre stood at the front of the kitchen, close to EJ, to address the girls. "So you think you can bake? We will see. In front of you are the ingredients for a simple cupcake. But do not be fooled, often the simplest thing is the hardest to perfect, and I want perfection. If I don't get it, you will go home. Now, enough chitty chatty, commence!"

EJ was nervous. She must not lose. She must not be sent home. She hadn't even begun her mission. She looked at the ingredients: flour, eggs, sugar, cream, chocolate, pretty much the same as at Isi's house. She looked at the recipe. Simple enough. Certainly the other contestants seemed to think so, for they were all well underway with their mixing.

First she needed to melt some chocolate and cream. *How hard can that be?* she thought. She followed the instructions, putting some water in a saucepan and bringing it to a boil. She then tipped the cream and chocolate into a bowl and put the bowl into the saucepan, being careful that the water did not touch the sides. Soon, the boiling water began melting the chocolate. So far, so good.

Brriinngg Brriinngg

A phone rang in Madame Ombre's office, at the

front of the kitchen.

"Keep baking and no chitty chatty, I can see you all," cried Madame Ombre, as she strode into the office. Through the glass, EJ could see Madame Ombre talking animatedly, angrily.

Hmm, something has really whipped her into an even worse temper, thought EJ. *I need to find out what.* EJ took her chocolate charm from her bracelet and twisted. Seconds later she was holding what looked like a little chocolate bar. Remembering her briefing, EJ separated the first two rows. But how was she going to get the transmitter into Madame Ombre's office?

Suddenly, and luckily, for EJ at least, there was a crash as one of the contestants dropped a glass bowl. Madame Ombre had slammed the phone down and was out of her office in a flash.

"Who is making such a noise in my kitchen?" she fumed, as she stormed to the back of the kitchen where the poor girl was desperately trying to pick up pieces of glass.

EJ took her chance. She had only seconds.

While Madame Ombre, with her back turned, began to berate the girl in front of the other shocked contestants, EJ slipped into the office. She left the choc charm on Madam Ombre's desk. She placed it next to some other chocolates already lying there— the choc charm would go unnoticed. She hoped.

EJ left the office and quickly returned to her workstation. Madame Ombre was still yelling at the poor girl. It was then that EJ saw her saucepan. She had left it on the stove and the water had boiled over and into the chocolate and cream batter. EJ was dismayed as she looked at the watery slop that was supposed to be her creamy chocolate. It was ruined. She looked back at Madame Ombre who was now almost exploding with rage.

"No, you butterfingers, this will not do. You cannot break things in my kitchen. You will have to leave the Choc Chef competition. Now. Someone will show you out. *Au revoir.* And the rest of you, you are warned, no mistakes!"

The other contestants watched in shocked silence as the now teary girl was escorted out of the competition. EJ looked back at her own mistake in the saucepan. She needed to hide it before Madame Ombre saw it and threw her out of the competition as well. Madame Ombre was now storming back toward the front of the kitchen, toward EJ and her chocolate water. EJ held her breath.

Brriinngg Brriinngg

The phone was ringing again. Madame Ombre let out an exasperated *"Ou la la la!"* as she stomped back into her office. "The things I must put up with!"

EJ let out a sigh of relief. She was saved again, but she couldn't keep counting on phones ringing to save her. She would have to do better. She quickly opened up the cupboard under her workstation and took out a new bowl, stuffing the bowl with the ruined batter in the cupboard, right at the back.

EJ needed to start her batter again, but she also needed to listen in to Madame Ombre's phone call. She took out the choc charm listening blocks and, as she put a new batch of chocolate into the new bowl, she held the choc charm close to her ear. She could hear Madame Ombre talking.

"*Non,* it cannot be sent out today… *Non,* it is not possible, it is not safe. The cakes are not finished. I have children everywhere and the TV cameras will be here later. We cannot change the cake delivery day."

Cake delivery? thought EJ. *The S6 cakes?*

Madame Ombre was talking again. "*Oui, oui,* but I do not like these little shadow people changing things; if I must send out today, you must give me more flakes. If they are not in my office in one hour I will not send out today."

EJ smiled to herself. *Shadow people, flakes. Are these the same flakes as in the coded message? Was Madame Ombre talking about sending out S6?* she thought.

"*Oui,*" continued Madame Ombre. "What do I care? You get me my flakes, I send you your cakes. *Au revoir.*" Madame Ombre hung up the phone and hurried out of the office and into the kitchen, calling out to the contestants as she did.

"You have used up half your time. If your cupcakes are not soon in the oven, I think you will be going home. I shall return shortly. No chitty chatty!"

I bet I know where she is going, thought EJ. *The storeroom. That's where I need to be, but I have to make these cakes.*

Now, more than a little flustered, EJ put the choc charm in her pocket and turned the stove back on to melt the second batch of cream and chocolate. She looked around at the other contestants. They were already lining their cupcake pans. While EJ had discovered important information, she was now running behind in the competition.

All around her was the clanging of saucepans and baking sheets as the contestants were preparing their cupcakes for baking. EJ, however, was preparing to worry: she was way behind. She may have finally gotten the chocolate and cream ready, but that was only part of the batter. She thought now was a reasonable time to panic.

Then the girl cooking at the workstation next to EJ smiled at her. It was the same girl who had smiled at her in the sculpting room. EJ smiled back.

"That was really mean, what Madame Ombre did," whispered the girl.

"I know," said EJ. "Scary."

"I'm Chloe," said the girl, still smiling as she rather expertly cracked an egg with one hand.

Chloe, thought EJ. *Might this be CC12?*

Chloe cracked another egg as she whispered again. "I really like chocolate, don't you?"

It was CC12! EJ was excited and she rushed to the next line of the exchange.

"Oh yes, especially white chocolate—have you tried it with grated carrot?"

"With what?" exclaimed Chloe. "That's funny." She giggled as she turned back to her cupcakes.

"Oh well, it's kind of nice," muttered EJ, not sounding very convincing, but feeling very embarrassed. Chloe was obviously not CC12. Then EJ realized that Chloe had not given the password exactly—she hadn't said, "I like chocolate very much, do you?" EJ felt bad. She might have blown her cover. At the moment she was being both a bad chef and a bad special agent. Now was a really good time to panic.

EJ quickly broke her eggs into a bowl, added the sugar and plugged in the electric mixer. As the beaters whirred away, mixing the eggs and sugar, EJ began to worry about the next stage, the real mixing stage, the potentially lumpy stage.

Trying not to stress, EJ started to measure out the dry ingredients, first the flour, then the baking powder, sugar and cocoa powder. Her cakes needed to be light and fluffy, but EJ was feeling anything but light. Her heart was thumping and her tummy was tightening. EJ was starting to worry that she was going to mess everything up. *Pull yourself together,* she told herself, *lighten up.* "Lighten up," that made EJ think of Isi. Maybe she could help EJ calm down? Checking that no one was looking, EJ took out her phone. Under the counter, she switched it to vibrate and sent Isi a text message.

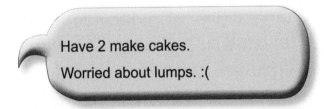

Have 2 make cakes.

Worried about lumps. :(

Within seconds, Isi, being on mission alert, had sent a text back.

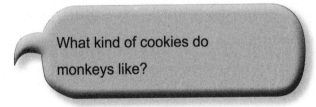

What kind of cookies do

monkeys like?

This was not the kind of mission assist EJ was expecting, but then she knew to expect the unexpected with Isi. She smiled and already felt herself growing calmer. Having a nutty friend could be useful. She sent a text back.

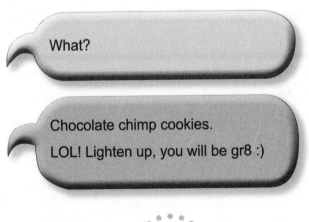

What?

Chocolate chimp cookies.

LOL! Lighten up, you will be gr8 :)

EJ started to laugh and, as she did, she noticed there was flour sprinkled all over her workstation. EJ looked closer. There seemed to be something written in the flour.

CC? Is it Agent CC12? wondered EJ. She had already been wrong once. But no, it had to be her and this time EJ would be more careful with the password. She put her phone back in her pocket and looked around the kitchen. Madame Ombre still hadn't returned.

Excellent! thought EJ, as she left her workstation and went over to the cool room, a room like a giant fridge. EJ opened the door and looked around.

She could see lots of ingredients—cream, milk, butter, boxes of fruit—but that was all. If Agent CC12 was hiding, she wouldn't give away her location unless she was sure it was another **SHINE** agent who had entered the cool room. There was only one way EJ could let her know.

She cleared her throat and facing the fruit announced, "I like chocolate very much, do you?"

Then EJ heard a voice from behind the bananas.

"Oh yes, especially white chocolate—have you tried it with grated carrot?"

Chapter • 10

EJ stood in the cool room and said the next part of the secret password to a box of bananas.

"No, I have only had it with tomato. I hope to try carrot soon."

"Yes," came the voice behind the bananas, "you must."

The sequence had been completed exactly.

"Agent CC12?" whispered EJ. "Is that you?"

"Affirmative, Agent EJ12."

EJ moved a box of bananas to one side and there, sitting cross-legged in among the fruit, was a girl. She seemed shorter than EJ, but apart from that looked about the same age. She had reddish-blond hair tied back in braids, pale skin and friendly looking blue eyes.

"You took your time; I was getting cold in here!"

"Sorry," replied EJ. "I've been a bit busy and I only just got your message in the flour. How did you manage to hide in here?"

"I came in with the fruit delivery this morning."

"Cool," smiled EJ, for a moment wishing she could be in the surveillance division. "CC12, what have you learned?"

"Madame Ombre is working for *SHADOW*," said CC, "and she has been baking lots more cupcakes than usual."

"Interesting that it's cupcakes she has been baking," said EJ, and she filled in CC on the message she had decoded that morning.

"Sneaky," said CC, "a message on a cupcake."

"Yes," continued EJ. "The message said the S6 cakes would be ready after the Junior Choc Chef finals, but I've just overheard Madame Ombre on the phone. I'm pretty sure that there is a change of plans and now they're going to be delivered today."

"That's bad," said CC, "we don't know enough yet."

"There's another thing," said EJ. "Have you seen or heard anything about flakes?"

"Flakes?" asked CC.

"Yes, flakes, Madame Ombre seems to be working with *SHADOW* for flakes and I am pretty sure she is not talking about cornflakes."

CC screwed up her nose. "I don't know what they are, but I do know that Madame Ombre has been planning what she hopes will be her best cake ever and that she is waiting on a delivery to start it. She could be waiting on the flakes."

"I think you're right," said EJ. She had a feeling that the pieces were starting to come together. "And I am pretty sure something is going on in that storeroom near the kitchen. Madame Ombre is the only person allowed in there."

"Yes," confirmed CC, "and she has been taking trays and trays of cupcakes in there over the last five days. I haven't seen them come out again."

"We need to get in there," said EJ.

"There will be a break after this first baking round. Use your skeleton key charm to get in and meet me in the storeroom."

"Okay, but first I need to make sure I get to the next round, otherwise I won't be going anywhere except home."

"You don't have a charm?" asked CC.

EJ remembered her whisk charm. "You're right, thanks. I'd better get out there and use it."

"I can hear someone coming!" whispered CC. "Move the banana box back and I will see you in the storeroom. Quick, now!"

EJ moved the box back and as she did, Madame Ombre opened the door of the cool room.

"What are you doing in here?" she asked, glaring at EJ.

"I'm just getting some more cream," replied EJ a little nervously. "Ah, here it is, thank you." EJ walked past Madame Ombre, who was still glaring, and back to her workstation. *Does Madame Ombre suspect something?* wondered EJ. As she opened the cream, she saw that most of the other contestants were already putting their cakes into the oven.

This charm better be good, thought EJ. She took out the whisk charm and twisted. As she did, it expanded to nearly ten times its original size and EJ noticed a little green button on the handle. She tipped the cream and chocolate into the eggs-and-sugar batter and then pushed the button on the whisk and put it into the bowl. If you listened carefully, you could hear a whirring noise coming from the whisk-o-matic and every now and then, EJ could hear a little "puff" as the whisk added something to the batter. Whatever it was, it was working, and EJ watched with relief as her batter became silky smooth without a lump to be seen.

Next EJ tipped the dry ingredients into the bowl. Her face fell when she saw her beautiful batter turn all lumpy, but with the whisk-o-matic whirring and puffing away, the batter was soon back to its silklike texture.

EJ carefully poured the batter into the cupcake

pans and put them into the oven. They looked good, but would they come out okay?

With the cakes in the oven, EJ twisted the top of the whisk-o-matic and it returned, slightly stickier, to its charm form. She began to clean up and waited nervously as the cakes baked. Finally, there was a ping as EJ's oven timer went off. She opened the door and peered nervously into the oven. To her surprise and delight, there was a tray of perfectly smooth and round cupcakes.

Madame Ombre rang a bell. "I am ready to judge. Choc Chefs, present your cupcakes!"

EJ looked at her cakes now cooling on the rack. They looked perfect—but how would they taste? Would they be good enough? She was about to find out.

"Ugh, that is not a cupcake, that is a disgrace. *Au revoir!*" declared Madame Ombre, as she tried one of the contestants' cakes. The girl began to blush. EJ felt sorry for her.

"That one is okay," said Madame Ombre to the next contestant. "That is very nice, that is too heavy," she said. Madame Ombre worked her way down the kitchen, making comments, some good, some bad, some quite rude. She came, at last, to EJ.

"Well, what about you? What did you do with your extra cream I wonder?" said Madame Ombre.

EJ held her breath as Madame Ombre took a cupcake and sliced it in half before putting one half into her mouth. She looked surprised, looked at EJ and then looked at the remaining half cupcake before putting that into her mouth as well. "That—" she said loudly.

EJ's heart sank. *She was going home, she knew it. What would she say to A1?*

"—that is the best cupcake of the contest. I am surprised—and impressed. Welcome to the final four!"

EJ breathed out. She—and her whisk-o-matic— had made it into the finals. Now, more importantly, she had to make it into that secret room.

Chapter • 11

The six unlucky contestants had left the kitchen and Madame Ombre now addressed the final four.

"The cakes must be completely cool before they can be decorated," said Madame Ombre. "While you wait you will be lucky enough to see a special feature film, *'Chocolat et Moi;* The Story of Madame Ombre and Her Remarkable Chocolate Cakes.' This will be a treat, I am sure you agree. We will go now to my theatrette, where you will stay and watch until I come to get you."

EJ smiled. This would be her opportunity to

sneak to the storeroom. She went with the others to the tiny theater and took a seat at the very back, close to the door. The lights dimmed and Madame Ombre left as the movie began to play. EJ waited a few moments before she too left the room. Poking her head around the door, she checked that Madame Ombre had gone, then went out into the main corridor and made her way to the storeroom. EJ took her key charm and twisted it. Once the key was fully extended, she pushed it into the keyhole and turned. The door was unlocked and, with a quick look up and down the corridor, EJ went inside. It was dark, but she dared not turn on the light.

"EJ12, over here!" A flashlight shone on the other side of the room. It was CC12.

"CC12, we have about an hour before the movie finishes and the finals commence. I'm not sure where Madame Ombre is."

"She is in the chocolate room, for now anyway. Look, EJ," said CC shining her flashlight. "I think we've found something."

CC shone her flashlight into the center of the

room and over an enormous table stacked high with cupcakes in plastic packing trays. In each tray there were spaces for six cakes, but there were only five cupcakes packed. Every tray was the same, five cupcakes and an empty space.

"There's one cupcake missing in every pack, that's strange," said EJ.

"Too much of a coincidence for it to be accidental," agreed CC.

"And," said EJ, "we're looking for a delivery of S6 cakes and here are delivery packs for six cakes. That can't be a coincidence either, can it?"

"I can see why you are in the code division," said CC.

"Thanks," replied EJ. "Let's have a closer look at these cupcakes."

They each took a cupcake and looked at it, closely, upside down, right way up. They looked normal enough. And delicious.

"There has to be something about these cakes," said EJ, "but what?"

"Maybe… shush! What was that?" CC whispered.

EJ couldn't hear anything. "What did you hear?" EJ whispered back.

"That," said CC.

Now EJ could hear it. There was a noise coming from the corner of the room, a rustling, shuffling kind of noise.

CC shone her flashlight into the corner. "Boxes, piles of boxes," she said.

"But boxes don't rustle," said EJ. "There has to be something else there."

The two girls walked up to the boxes with CC shining her flashlight on them. The rustling seemed louder. EJ reached up and lifted one of the surprisingly light boxes and put it on the floor. CC took the next one and both girls gasped when they saw what was behind the boxes.

"Rabbits," said CC.

Along the back wall was a cage holding six rabbits. The lovely brown rabbits EJ had seen in the sculpting room.

"Madame Ombre's chocolate models," said EJ. "How cruel to keep them locked up in here in the dark behind all these boxes."

It was when EJ looked down at the boxes that she noticed a label.

> **Deliver to:**
> **Madame Ombre Chocolate Bakery**
> **Bottom Up First**
>
> **Contents:** 6 Cartons
> Sugar
> Lemons
> Apples
> Nuts
> Icing
> Figs

"What a strange combination of contents," said EJ. "Too strange, I think."

"What do you mean?" asked CC.

"I think it's a code," replied EJ. "But what sort of code is it? Let me see, there is always a clue to the code somewhere. Maybe here: *Bottom Up First*. Maybe it's something about the first letter." EJ took out her phone and pressed the notes app. She keyed in the first letter of each line:

```
6SLANIF
```

"Maybe not," said EJ a little glumly.

"But 6S, is that something?" asked CC.

"Yes!" cried EJ, as she remembered back to the first cupcake code where she got 6S wrong. "It is S6 and I didn't use the whole clue: 'Bottom Up First.' We need to take the first letters from the bottom. Look." EJ keyed in another set of letters.

```
FINAL S6
```

"The contents of this box are the final part of S6. Maybe that's why the last cake isn't in the tray? I wonder. Let's open the box."

The girls took down the box and opened it. Inside were lots of little plastic bags, each with what looked like a single chocolate chip in them.

"S6 is a chocolate chip? Maybe we have gotten this all wrong," said CC.

"We can't have." EJ looked closely at the chip. "It has to be something else as well. Something hidden maybe."

"We need to be hidden as well," said CC quickly. "I can hear something else, and it's not rabbits."

"I can't hear anything," said EJ, wondering if agents in the surveillance division had to have really good hearing.

"Trust me, EJ!" whispered CC. "Quick, up here."

EJ followed CC as the nimble girl climbed up over the boxes and down over the other side next to the rabbits. Just before EJ jumped down she took her cupcake charm and twisted it. "This should help us," she whispered, as she removed the cherry camera and placed it on the top of the highest box, looking down over the large table. Now she could hear something too. Footsteps. And the door opening.

The light went on. Both girls held their breath.

Behind the boxes, both girls took out their phones and pressed the **SHINE** Chat app. Using **SHINE** Chat they could text each other. EJ activated cupcake-cam and they watched the screen showing Madame Ombre come into the room. She was carrying a baking sheet of cakes and what looked like a paint can and brush. She put both on the large table. Carefully Madame Ombre took one of the cupcakes on her tray and sliced off the peaked top of the cake. The girls watched as she then took a small scoop out of the middle of the cake and looked around.

"Now, where are my chips?" she wondered aloud.

EJ froze and quickly wrote a message:

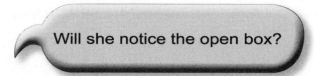

Will she notice the open box?

A second later a message from CC appeared on EJ's screen.

We will soon find out.

"Ah, there they are." Madame Ombre saw the opened box on the end of the table. "Yes, let me check. Final S6, the chocolate chip microchip." Madame Ombre dropped the chip into the center of the cake, placed the top of the cake back on and then seemed to paint something brown over the top.

"The icing on the cake, chocolate icing," Madame Ombre said chuckling to herself. "A little icing seals the cake and the chip inside. Madame, you are indeed a master chef!"

CC sent EJ another text.

Master evil chef.

EJ smiled. It was fun having a mission partner for a change.

The two agents continued to watch on cupcake-cam as Madame Ombre inserted a chip into each cake on her baking sheet, replacing the top and icing them over. She put one into each of the packing trays and, with the pack complete, she sealed the packs.

"One more batch of cakes and all the packs will be completed. *SHADOW* will have their cakes and I will have my flakes. I will soon have enough to begin my ultimate creation."

EJ sent CC a text.

You were right!

Madame Ombre got up from the table and moved to the other side of the room. There, in the corner, was a large safe. EJ and CC hadn't noticed it in the dark, but now they watched as Madame Ombre keyed in a code and opened a thick black door. Madame Ombre took out a gold box, almost cradling it as if it were a baby.

"My beautiful gold flakes," said Madame Ombre, gently lifting out what looked like thin gold paper. "Soon I will have enough for the golden chocolate cake that will make me the most famous chef in the world. But enough chitty chatty, I must check that my final delivery of flakes has arrived, and I need more cakes. I must have them all finished before I have to go back to those pesky kids and watch their no doubt awful decorating work."

And with that Madame Ombre left. EJ and CC heard the door shutting and then footsteps walking away.

The girls climbed back out over the boxes, EJ picking up the cupcake-cam cherry as she did.

"She's crazy," said EJ. "Helping *SHADOW* so she can make a cake? But she is clever. There are six components to make one S6 and she is hiding one component in each cake. A full tray of cakes makes one S6."

"Let's make sure," said CC and they broke open one of the cupcakes. Then another, and another until they had opened all six cupcakes in a pack. "Yes! Look, there is a small part in each cake, but you would never know it was there if you didn't know what to look for. It just looks as if a pack of chocolate-iced cupcakes are being delivered. And they are delicious," she added, taking a pinch of cake.

"They are," agreed EJ, also taking a pinch. "We thought the '6' just stood for the six words,

SHADOW Secret Scramble Send and Spy System, but it also means it comes in six parts."

"And she is sending out all these trays," said CC, indicating the piles of cupcake trays on the table. "That's a lot of *SHADOW* agents."

"We need a plan to stop these cupcakes going out," said EJ.

"And quickly," replied CC. "Madame Ombre will soon be back with the last batch of cakes and then they'll be sent out. Let's call **SHINE**."

Chapter • 12

EJ had barely finished keying in the number when A1 answered. EJ quickly told her what she and CC had learned.

"You have done well, girls, but we still have a bit to do. We need the S6, but we also need to see where it is being delivered. CC?"

"Yes, A1?"

"You need to bring us S6. Our chopper will be waiting for you on the roof of the bakery. Use the escape route."

"Check," replied CC confidently.

"EJ," said A1, "you need to stay there for just

a little longer. You can't suddenly leave. It will look suspicious if you don't compete in the final. We also need you to do a few more things. First, we need you to put the cherry on top of Madame Ombre's cupcakes."

"Pardon?" asked EJ, confused.

"The cherry from the cupcake-cam is also a homing device. If you can put that on a cupcake containing S6 we will be able to follow the delivery truck as it leaves the bakery."

"I can do that," said EJ, just as confidently as CC. "I can do it now with a pack here. What next?"

"This one might be a bit harder. We need the gold flakes that *SHADOW* is paying Madame Ombre with. *SHADOW* stole them from the Institute of Cookery and we should return them."

"Okay," said EJ, sounding a little less sure. That would be harder. She would have to wait for the new delivery and then get the box of flakes out of the safe, a safe that could only be opened with a code. A code she didn't know.

"And EJ?" continued A1.

"Yes, A1," said EJ. *There can't be more, can there?* she thought.

"Good luck in the final. Good luck to both of you. **SHINE** out."

EJ carefully unsealed one of the packs of cupcakes and slid out the tray. She took the cherry from the cupcake-cam and placed it on a cupcake before resealing the pack. She then put a couple of other packs on top of the pack.

"No one will ever know it's there," she said to CC. "**SHINE** will be able to follow the delivery truck all the way to *SHADOW*."

"Good job, now let's go, EJ," said CC, grabbing the one complete pack of cupcakes. "We need to go to the bathroom!"

"I don't think I need to," replied EJ.

"No, not for that," said CC, giggling. "The escape route is in the bathroom."

"Right," said EJ, feeling a little embarrassed. "Let's go then."

EJ should have known. One way or another, she always seemed to spend some mission time in the bathroom. The girls ran quickly down the corridor and into the bathroom. While CC checked that no one else was there, EJ turned on the hand dryers. CC went into the last stall on the left.

"Come on," she called to EJ. "In here!" EJ followed CC in.

"Okay, this is the escape route. Look up, there's a ventilation fan. I am going to remove the fan and climb up through the hole, then crawl through the ventilation shaft and up onto the roof. The **SHINE** helicopter will pick me up from the roof."

"Cool, CC," replied EJ, "Hey, CC with cc!"

"Pardon?" said CC.

"CC with cupcakes," replied EJ.

"You code girls think too much!" laughed CC. "Hey, you do have a rope climbing charm don't you?"

"Only a glow rope, I think," said EJ, quickly checking her bracelet.

"Okay, wait for me to climb up and then you can borrow mine. You'll need to escape this way once you have the gold."

CC took a charm from her bracelet, twisted it,

and was soon holding a rope with a hook on the end. She stood up on the toilet tank and pushed the fan out with the toilet brush holder.

"It's glamorous, this spy business, isn't it?" said CC, as she threw her rope up through the fan hole. She heard the hook catch, gave the rope a tug to make sure it was firmly in place, and then began to climb up the stall wall. Once up through the hole, she stuck her head back down and held out the rope charm to EJ. "Here's the charm. Good luck, EJ12."

"You too, CC12. See you soon," replied EJ.

CC put the fan back over the hole and was gone. EJ flushed the toilet, just in case anyone was coming in, opened the stall door and walked out of the bathroom. She checked the time on her phone. She had been gone for nearly an hour. The movie would soon finish. EJ needed to hurry.

EJ sneaked back into the little theater, sitting down just as the movie was ending. Madame Ombre appeared at the door. *That was close,* EJ thought.

"And so," Madame Ombre cried, "let the finals begin. To the Choc Chef kitchen!"

She led EJ and the three other finalists back into the kitchen where their cakes were laid out ready for the final. At the back of the kitchen a TV crew was setting up their equipment.

"And so," said Madame Ombre, "you have just thirty minutes to decorate your cakes and arrange them on the display. I will then decide who will be the Junior Choc Chef, live on TV."

The girls looked at each other, smiling.

"Your time starts now!"

Madame Ombre went into her office and came out holding a package. She then left the kitchen.

That could be the gold, thought EJ. *She's taking it to add to the box in the safe. I need to decorate these cakes and get back there too. But when?*

She started on her cakes, but had no time to worry about what they looked like. EJ quickly iced the cakes with the chocolate icing on the table and began almost throwing decorations onto them—

sprinkles, snakes, chocolate stars, anything.

Madame Ombre returned to the kitchen and began pacing the workstations. She glanced at EJ's cakes and frowned. She then looked at EJ and frowned again.

Somehow I don't think I am going to win, thought EJ, but she wasn't worried, she had her mind on a much bigger prize.

Madame Ombre returned to her office and picked up her phone. EJ switched on the choc-charm receiver. The transmitter was still in Madame Ombre's office.

"Yes, trash disposal? Make sure you take the rabbits when you clean tonight. I will leave them in the corridor. What to do with them? I do not know what to do with them. I am a baker, not a rabbit farmer. I needed them to model for Easter bunnies and now I don't need them anymore. Take them away! *Au revoir.*"

EJ could hear Madame Ombre slam her phone down. *How could she simply throw out the rabbits? They were live animals, not trash.* EJ couldn't let that happen and started to think of a rescue plan as she placed the cakes on the tiered display plates. Then she felt her phone vibrate. Pretending to look for something in the cupboard, she checked her phone. It was a message from **SHINE**.

> LEAVE BAKERY WITH GOLD NOW. HAVE INTERCEPTED EMAIL FROM *SHADOW* TO MO. THEY KNOW THERE WAS NO EMMA SEKAC IN THE PRELIMINARY ROUNDS OF JUNIOR CHOC CHEF. THEY WILL SOON CHECK WHY MO HAS NOT REPLIED TO THE EMAIL.

Just as Madame Ombre opened the door of her office to leave, the phone rang again. She shut the door and turned toward the phone. EJ knew that Emma Sekac's time in the Junior Choc Chef finals was up. She ran.

Chapter •13

As fast as she could, EJ ran back to the storeroom and opened the door with her skeleton key. The door opened and she rushed over to the safe. Next to the safe was the package she had seen Madame Ombre take out of the kitchen. It was empty. *I bet she has put whatever was in there in the safe,* thought EJ. *I need to open this safe.*

She had little time as she knew Madame Ombre would be looking for her. The safe had a keypad, a simple letter–number pad like a phone, on which to enter a code to open it. But there were thousands of possible combinations.

Think, EJ, think, she said to herself. And then she remembered that she and CC had watched Madame Ombre keying a code on the cupcake-cam.

That's it! thought EJ to herself. *I can watch it again on playback. Maybe I'll be able to see the code she keyed in?*

She took out the cupcake-cam and pressed rewind. When she found the right footage, she pressed slow motion playback. At the same time she zoomed in on Madame Ombre's fingers as she keyed in the code.

Aarrghh, thought EJ, *I can't see it, it's too blurry.* She pressed back, and played it again. She still couldn't see what Madame Ombre had keyed, but she could see that she keyed in eight numbers. Eight numbers, but which ones? EJ didn't have a lot of time for guesses: Madame Ombre would find her any minute.

Just then EJ's phone vibrated. It was a text from Isi.

Hope all good. Have just bought us each a button. Here's a pic :)

chocolate is the answer

Isi, you are a genius, thought EJ. Madame Ombre keyed in letters, not numbers. "Chocolate" is what she keyed in—what else would Madame Ombre have as a code?

EJ began to key in the letters, but nothing happened.

Dumb! C-h-o-c-o-l-a-t-e. That's nine letters and the code is eight so that can't be it.

Then EJ heard footsteps, hurried footsteps that were getting louder. She heard Madame Ombre shouting in French.

French, EJ thought, *that's it! Wouldn't Madame Ombre do her code in French? What is chocolate in French? What had Madame Ombre said when she greeted them? Was it* chocolat? *But how did you spell that in French?*

EJ quickly opened the translator app on her phone and keyed in chocolate. She smiled as she saw the answer.

> CHOCOLAT

Chocolat. *No "e" and that makes it eight letters. Yes! Or should that be* Oui!

EJ keyed in C-H-O-C-O-L-A-T and tried the handle. The safe door opened. EJ reached in and grabbed the small gold box and opened it. It was filled with gold—gold flakes.

"Gotcha," said EJ.

But then she heard the footsteps again and this time they were really close. EJ hid behind the boxes, holding her breath. She waited for the door to open.

It didn't. The footsteps went straight past the storeroom.

EJ was relieved, but knew it wouldn't be long before Madame Ombre checked the storeroom.

EJ needed to get out quickly, but she couldn't leave without the rabbits. She looked at the bunnies huddled in the cage and knew she couldn't abandon them to be put out with the trash. But how was EJ going to carry six rabbits? There had to be something in the room that she could use to carry them. EJ scanned the room. Flour. Of course a bakery had flour and what did flour come in? Bags. Big bags and they were all stacked up in the corner next to the rabbit cage. There was only one problem, the bags were, not surprisingly, full of flour.

EJ didn't have much time. She quickly flicked through her charms for something that would open the bags. *Crocodile repellent, no, penguin food, no. Maybe this,* she thought, as she saw the hook from CC's rope charm. *That might work.* EJ quickly twisted the rope charm. Once it had enlarged, she grabbed the hook and thrust it into the corner of a flour bag and pulled it back toward her. The bag ripped open and flour spilled out. EJ shrunk the rope back to its charm size, then tipped the bag upside down and, as even more flour went everywhere, she opened the rabbit cage and gently lifted each now rather white rabbit into the bag.

"Don't worry, little ones. You won't be in there for long," said EJ.

"*Non*, not long at all," said a voice behind EJ. A French voice.

It was Madame Ombre.

EJ, with the box of gold flakes in one hand and a sack of rabbits in the other, froze in front of a very cross and now quite scary-looking Madame Ombre. *"I'll take the gold box,* Emma Sekac, or should that be EJ12?" snarled Madame Ombre. "You won't be going anywhere."

"It's too late, Madame Ombre. **SHINE** already knows about *SHADOW* and S6."

"Do you think I care about *SHADOW* and their silly S6? *Non*, just give me my gold flakes. Now," said Madame Ombre, glaring threateningly at EJ.

EJ looked straight at Madame Ombre and saw

the "First comes chocolate" on her jacket. *She will do anything for her chocolate cakes,* realized EJ, *and that gives me an idea.* She put the rabbit bag down gently and opened the box of gold flakes. She held up some of the fragile flakes.

"You mean these?" asked EJ.

"Be careful, you fool. They will fall out. Do you have any idea how rare edible 24-carat gold flakes are?"

EJ took out some more. She could see how much this was worrying Madame Ombre. She wanted her gold flakes a lot more than she wanted a pesky **SHINE** agent.

She blew some of the flakes out of her hand. Madame Ombre dropped to the floor and picked them up. "Don't do that again, you fool, you will ruin them. Now give them to me."

"What, like this?" This time EJ turned away from Madame Ombre, then grabbed a whole handful of flakes and threw them high up into the air, hoping her plan would work.

It did. Madame Ombre moved like a shot from

114

the door past EJ to where the flakes had fallen at the back of the room. She dropped to her knees to pick them up. As she did, EJ took another handful of gold, put the lid on the box, picked up her bag of bunnies and sprinted for the door.

But would she make it to the escape route?

"Come back with my gold!" yelled Madame Ombre.

Chapter •14

EJ had never run so fast and, as she ran, she scattered more handfuls of gold flakes on the floor.

That should slow her down, she hoped.

EJ reached the bathroom. She turned back and could see Madame Ombre behind her, but the chef kept stopping to pick up the gold. EJ pushed open the bathroom door, went straight to the last stall and climbed up on the toilet. She pushed the fan out of the way with the toilet brush and threw the box up into the shaft. EJ reactivated the climbing rope charm then threw the climbing hook through the opening, just as CC had, and pulled on it to check that it had caught. Quickly but carefully tying the other end of the rope around the rabbit bag, EJ pulled herself up into the shaft. *Thank goodness for gymnastics,* EJ thought. *I need every arm and tummy muscle I've got.*

Once she was up, she pulled up the rabbit bag and the rope. Just as she lifted the bag into the shaft, she heard the bathroom door crash open. Madame Ombre appeared in the stall. Now she looked very scary.

"Give me my gold!" she shrieked.

EJ poked her head through the opening. "Enough chitty chatty, must fly," said EJ. *"Au revoir!"*

With Madame Ombre's furious screams ringing in her ears, EJ crawled along the ventilator shaft toward the roof, pushing the boxes in front of her and pulling the bunnies.

"Not long to go now, guys," she said soothingly.

At the end of the ventilation shaft there was a door. EJ pushed it open and climbed onto the roof of the bakery. In the distance, she could see the lights of the **SHINE** chopper, waiting for her.

EJ waved her arms and it sped toward her. As it hovered above the roof, a rope was lowered from the chopper. EJ first tied the gold box securely and gave the thumbs-up. The rope was raised and then lowered again, this time for EJ. And her precious cargo.

"Hold on," she said to the rabbits. "Going up!"

EJ was winched up to the chopper. At the door was CC, shouting at her.

"Way to go, EJ! Take my arm."

EJ did and CC pulled her into the chopper. As she got her breath back, she smiled as she saw that Agent LP30 was once again the pilot.

"Good job, EJ12," said LP30. "It's time to go home."

With the chopper door shut, EJ opened the bag to let the rabbits have some air. Six little heads cautiously popped out, their noses twitching nervously.

"EJ12, can't you complete a mission without

bringing home animals?" exclaimed LP30.

"It's not my fault, I couldn't leave them there," explained EJ. "Madame Ombre was going to throw them out with the trash."

"You did the right thing," said LP30. "I am sure we can find them good homes."

EJ rather hoped one of those good homes would be hers.

"EJ and CC, I have A1 on speakerphone," said LP30. "Go ahead, A1."

"Hello there, Agents EJ and CC, and well done. If you look at the screen in front of you, you will see the announcement of Junior Choc Chef on TV."

The girls watched as a very angry-looking Madame Ombre declared Chloe the Junior Choc Chef winner: she had turned her cupcake into the Sydney Opera House, complete with a seagull on top. *And*, EJ wondered, as she looked closely, *was that a little bit of grated carrot on the white chocolate?*

"Bad luck that you didn't win," said CC.

"I think we did," said EJ. "Oh, and," she added,

as she passed a charm to CC, "thanks for the loan of the rope."

"You certainly did win," broke in A1. "Thanks to the cherry homing device, a **SHINE** team is following Madame Ombre's delivery truck as we speak. Not only do we have S6, but we will soon have all the delivery addresses of the *SHADOW* agents. I call that having your cake and eating it too!"

"A1, could I ask a favor?" said EJ. "You know the whisk-o-matic?"

"Yes," said A1 guardedly.

"Well, I know we are not supposed to use mission charms in normal life, but I was just wondering if you might make an exception just once, for a really good cause."

"I know about your fund-raiser, EJ, and yes, I think just this once that might be possible."

"Thanks, A1," said EJ. The fund-raiser reminded her about Isi. She hadn't really used her BESTie that much this mission, but Isi had been there for her.

EJ took out her phone. As she went to text her friend she noticed the little heart charm. She hadn't used that either. She gave it a twist and the inscription appeared

Lighten up and laugh.

That could have been Isi's motto. EJ texted her friend.

> Nearly home, thx for help.

> I didn't do anything.

> You did more than you think.

> In that case—why did the chocolate factory hire the farmer?

EJ showed CC the text and the two girls giggled for most of the ride home.

Chapter •15

It was the afternoon before Chocolate Lovers' Day and Emma was at Isi's house again. This time Emma had enjoyed getting the cakes ready. The girls had laughed and joked as they cooked and the cakes were now baking in the oven. While they waited, they played with Isi's new rabbit. Sadly, Emma hadn't succeeded in convincing her mother that she should have one, but she had not given up on her master plan for more animals. Meanwhile, Isi having one of the rabbits was nearly as fun and the animal shelter had helped Emma find good homes for the others.

"I just know these cakes will be so much better than last time, Em," said Isi. "The batter didn't have a single lump in it. How did we do that?"

"I have no idea," said Emma. And she really didn't because she had accidentally left the whisk-o-matic in her bag at home. *Maybe*, she thought, *I have lightened up?*

"Hey," said Isi, "did you hear that Madame Ombre has moved back to France? I guess that means we can't enter next year's Junior Choc Chef—and just as we seem to have gotten the hang of it."

They had indeed. The cupcakes were so light and fluffy they nearly bounced out of the oven. The girls had a ball decorating them with different candies and sprinkles.

And the next day at school the cakes sold out in the first half hour. Emma needn't have worried about not raising enough money for the shelter. Chocolate Lovers' Day was a huge and delicious success.

Ms. Tenga sent the money to the shelter and was thrilled to read aloud the email from the shelter director.

"'Thank you to all the students who raised so much money. I am happy to tell you that with your support, and that of so many other kind people, the animal shelter can continue its work helping animals. You are all shining stars.'"

Emma could have sworn that Ms. Tenga was looking at her when she said "shining stars," but she was so happy about the shelter that she didn't give it much thought.

"We did it, Em!" whispered Isi, grabbing her friend's hand. "We helped save the shelter."

"Yes, we did," said Emma, beaming back at her friend.

With, she thought to herself, *a little help from EJ12!*

Emma Jacks and EJ12 return in

BOOK 6
ON THE BALL

Have you read them all?

HOT & COLD

JUMP START

IN THE DARK

ROCKY ROAD

CHOC SHOCK

ON THE BALL

MAKING WAVES

DRAMA QUEEN